Flat Grandma

Written in memory of Andrea Marie Watts Sparling
Dedicated to young children and their grandmothers living far apart.

All profits from *Flat Grandma* go to The Andrea Watts Sparling Fund for Children,
a Donor Advised Fund of The Denver Foundation. www.denverfoundation.org

@ 2011 Edith Andersen

Emma is a little girl
who lives in a house with a backyard.
When she plays in the backyard
she smells the flowers
and goes mmmmm.

Emma has a mommy.
Her mommy has soft hands
that stroke her cheeks
and put bandaids on her knees
when she falls down.
My boo-boo still hurts.
I need another bandaid.
Emma tells her mommy.

Emma has a daddy.
Her daddy is a lot taller than Emma.
After he puts on her helmet with
the yellow teddy bears,
they ride to the park on his bicycle.
When they go fast, the wind
blows through her hair
and makes her laugh. Daddy tells her,
Hold on to the sides, Emma.

Emma has two dogs.
She has a big
brown dog, Doc.
She has a little
white dog, Billy.
She likes to grab Doc's
warm and wet nose.
Doc likes to lick her face.

When Emma is not putting hats
on Billy's soft and furry head,
he's running away with her doll.
Mommy, Billy, Billy
took my baby.
Stop Billy!

Emma has a flat grandma.
She lives in the computer. She has brown hair.
Her grandma wears glasses,
but Emma doesn't know if she wears shoes
because she can't see her feet.
When she reaches out to touch her grandma,
grandma feels cold and hard.

In the kitchen, Emma stands on a stool
to see grandma on the computer.
Billy sits on the floor.
He doesn't know how to talk to grandma.
Emma's grandma smiles at her and says,
Hi, Emma. I love you.

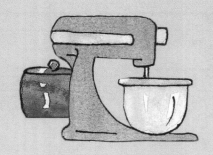

Emma and grandma play games.
They play hide-and-seek.
Where is Emma?
Grandma asks.
Mommy says,
Be careful on that stool.
Doc wants to go outside
and chase squirrels.

Sometimes grandma
reads a book to Emma.
Sometimes she puts a sock
on her hand and says,
This is a sock monster that eats daddies.
Emma laughs.
Grandma, socks only eat feet.

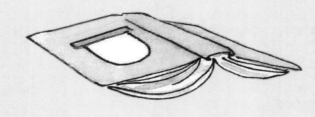

Emma reaches her arms out
to Grandma.
She wants grandma to hold her.
But her mommy says,
No Emma,
don't touch the computer.

One day, the doorbell rings.
Doc and Billy run to see
who is coming to the house.
Standing in the door is grandma.
Emma looks and looks.
Grandma got out of the computer!
She walks to grandma and touches her.
Grandma is soft and warm.

Grandma picks her up, gives her a big hug and whispers, *I love you very much, Emma.* Emma is happy that her flat grandma got out of the computer.